RAVEN

AND OTHER POEMS

20,000 Leagues Under the Sea
by Jules Verne
with an introduction by Bruce Coville

The Adventures of Tom Sawyer
by Mark Twain
with an introduction by Jean Craighead George

The Call of the Wild
by Jack London
with an introduction by Avi

A Christmas Carol
by Charles Dickens
with an introduction by Karen Hesse

Dracula
by Bram Stoker
with an introduction by Walter Dean Myers

A Little Princess
by Frances Hodgson Burnett
with an introduction by E.L. Konigsburg

Little Women
by Louisa May Alcott
with an introduction by Paula Danziger

Pride and Prejudice
by Jane Austen
with an introduction by Katherine Paterson

The Raven and Other Poems
by Edgar Allan Poe
with an introduction by Philip Pullman

The Secret Garden
by Frances Hodgson Burnett
with an introduction by Ann M. Martin

THE RAVEN AND OTHER POEMS

EDGAR ALLAN POE

With an introduction by Philip Pullman

SCHOLASTIC INC.
New York Toronto London Auckland
Sydney Mexico City New Delhi Hong Kong

If you purchased this book without a cover, you should be aware that this book is stolen property. It was reported as "unsold and destroyed" to the publisher, and neither the author nor the publisher has received any payment for this "stripped book."

No part of this publication may be reproduced, stored in a retrieval system, or transmitted in any form or by any means, electronic, mechanical, photocopying, recording, or otherwise, without written permission of the publisher. For information regarding permission, write to Scholastic Inc., Attention: Permissions Department, 557 Broadway, New York, NY 10012.

ISBN 978-0-439-22406-2

This edition copyright © 2000 by Scholastic Inc.
All rights reserved. Published by Scholastic Inc.
SCHOLASTIC and associated logos are trademarks and/or registered trademarks of Scholastic Inc.

12 11 10 9 8 7 12 13/0

Printed in the U.S.A. 23

INTRODUCTION

Once upon a midnight dreary . . .

How lucky you are, you who are about to read this poem for the first time.

I hope you read it when you're alone, at night, as I did when I first came across it.

I hope your flesh creeps and your skin crawls and the blood turns to ice in your veins.

I hope that your soul, like mine, will ever afterward be in thrall to that sinister, solemn word, the Raven's one mysterious message: "Nevermore!"

It was many and many a year ago, in a kingdom by the sea, that I first read "The Raven." I had read some of Poe's wonderful and gruesome short stories, and I thought the poem would be the same sort of thing, only in rhyme. I was partly right, because Poe's weird and intense world, half horror and half ecstasy, is the same all the way through; wherever you look, you find the same feeling.

But I hadn't expected the power of the verse. I hadn't expected to find my heart pounding, my fingers tapping, my whole body as excited by the rhythm of the words as by the rhythms of rock 'n' roll or jazz.

And here's a tip: Don't just read "The Raven," or any of these marvelous poems, with your eyes only. Take this book a long way away from everybody else, where you know no one can hear you, and read the poems aloud to yourself — a whisper will do, but you have to hear them. Read them with your mouth and your ears as well as your eyes. That's the only way to feel the extraordinary brilliance of the sound-patterns, the rhymes that lace the lines together, the incessant, insistent, merciless "tapping, as of someone gently rapping, rapping at my chamber door."

Read it aloud, and you'll be surprised to find how much of it sticks in your mind, and what a pleasure it is to take it out and play with it afterward.

Here's another tip. Don't worry about what it *means*. You don't need to know what a balm is, for example, or where to find Gilead to realize what's going on when those words turn up. The whole feeling of the verse tells you that it's something that the speaker longs for, hopes for, yearns for with all his soul, and we all know what that feels like; and we can all feel the deadly heart-crushing denial in the Raven's reply.

As a matter of fact, worrying about what poetry means takes most of the fun out of it. Teachers often forget this and think that the only way to enjoy a poem is to understand every single word, so they go through laboriously explaining and explaining and explaining, till the whole experience is a torment. Well, it's not true. Realizing that you don't have to *translate* it, and that you're allowed simply to say it to yourself and relish the taste and the shape and the color of these mysterious sounds, is the key to all poetry, not just Poe's. And the truly strange thing is that when you do that, it communicates anyway. Try it and see.

It's always tempting to look at a writer's work and try to find echoes of his or her life. Literal-minded readers often say that *this* story must have been based on *that* event; such-and-such a character is *obviously* a portrait of so-and-so; he *must* have been a drug addict because otherwise how could he know so much about it — and so on. It's all nonsense. Such literal-minded people forget that there's a faculty known as the imagination, with which writers and poets can bring to mind things they've never directly experienced and make them real for the rest of us. Poe had this faculty in abundance.

But like many other writers, he found himself returning to the same ideas over and over again, as if his imagination was drawn to them like a moth to a flame. One of Poe's obsessive themes was the death of a beautiful and beloved young woman. We find this in many of his stories, as well as in a number of poems here, not least "The Raven" itself. Look at "Annabel Lee"; look at my own favorite, the truly strange and unforgettable "Ulalume." This theme, the beautiful loved one dying young, did have a parallel in Poe's own life. In 1836, he married his cousin Virginia, who was only thirteen. He was a loving and devoted husband, and when, eleven years later, Virginia died of tuberculosis, it must have seemed to Poe that his most haunting stories were coming true.

"The Raven" was published in 1845, four years before Poe died. He was already quite well known as a critic and short-story writer, but the poem made him famous. It was soon known wherever poetry was read, and people have read it and loved it ever since. And if you haven't read it before, as I began by saying, how lucky you are; I envy you.

And I envy you your first encounter with "The Conqueror Worm" ("And much of Madness, and more of Sin, And Horror the soul of the plot"); and your first meeting with the beautiful Annabel Lee "In her sepulchre there by the sea,— In her tomb by the sounding sea"; and in "Ulalume" your first walk through the most creepy landscape in the whole of poetry, "down by the dank tarn of Auber, In the ghoul-haunted woodland of Weir."

But it's not only your first experience of this poetry that's enchanting. The magic lasts; the spell is permanent. Once these poems are in your head, they stay there for good. In fact, they leave you — Nevermore.

Philip Pullman
In the bleak December, 1999

CONTENTS

Dreams 11

The Lake 13

Sonnet — To Science 14

[Alone] 15

Introduction 16

To Helen 19

Israfel 20

The Valley of Unrest 23

The City in the Sea 24

To One in Paradise 26

The Coliseum 27

The Haunted Palace 29

The Conqueror Worm 31

Dream-Land 33

Eulalie 35

The Raven 36

["Deep in Earth"] 44

To M. L. S—— 45

Ulalume — A Ballad 46

The Bells 50

To Helen [Whitman] 54

A Dream Within a Dream 57

For Annie 58

Eldorado 62

To My Mother 63

Annabel Lee 64

Index of First Lines 67

Index of Poems 69

For Further Information 71

DREAMS

Oh! that my young life were a lasting dream!
My spirit not awak'ning till the beam
Of an Eternity should bring the morrow:
Yes! tho' that long dream were of hopeless
sorrow,
'Twere better than the dull reality
Of waking life to him whose heart shall be,
And hath been ever, on the chilly earth,
A chaos of deep passion from his birth!

But should it be — that dream eternally
Continuing — as dreams have been to me
In my young boyhood — should it thus be given,
'Twere folly still to hope for higher Heaven!
For I have revell'd, when the sun was bright
In the summer sky; in dreamy fields of light,
And left unheedingly my very heart
In climes of mine imagining — apart
From mine own home, with beings that have
been
Of mine own thought — what more could I have
seen?

"Twas once and *only* once and the wild hour
From my remembrance shall not pass — some
power
Or spell had bound me — 'twas the chilly wind
Came o'er me in the night and left behind

Its image on my spirit, or the moon
Shone on my slumbers in her lofty noon
Too coldly — or the stars — howe'er it was
That dream was as that night wind — let it
  pass.

I have been happy — tho' but in a dream.
I have been happy — and I love the theme —
Dreams! in their vivid colouring of life —
As in that fleeting, shadowy, misty strife
Of semblance with reality which brings
To the delirious eye more lovely things
Of Paradise and Love — and all our own!
Than young Hope in his sunniest hour hath
  known.

[1827–1828]

THE LAKE

In youth's spring, it was my lot
To haunt of the wide earth a spot
The which I could not love the less;
So lovely was the loneliness
Of a wild lake, with black rock bound,
And the tall trees that tower'd around.
But when the night had thrown her pall
Upon that spot — as upon all,
And the wind would pass me by
In its stilly melody,
My infant spirit would awake
To the terror of the lone lake.
Yet that terror was not fright —
But a tremulous delight,
And a feeling undefin'd,
Springing from a darken'd mind.
Death was in that poison'd wave
And in its gulf a fitting grave
For him who thence could solace bring
To his dark imagining;
Whose wild'ring thought could even make
An Eden of that dim lake.

[1827]

SONNET — TO SCIENCE

Science! true daughter of Old Time thou art!
  Who alterest all things with thy peering eyes.
Why preyest thou thus upon the poet's heart,
  Vulture, whose wings are dull realities?
How should he love thee? or how deem thee wise,
  Who wouldst not leave him in his wandering
To seek for treasure in the jewelled skies,
  Albeit he soared with an undaunted wing?
Hast thou not dragged Diana from her car?
  And driven the Hamadryad from the wood
To seek a shelter in some happier star?
  Hast thou not torn the Naiad from her flood,
The Elfin from the green grass, and from me
The summer dream beneath the tamarind tree?

[1829–1843]

[ALONE]

From childhood's hour I have not been
As others were — I have not seen
As others saw — I could not bring
My passions from a common spring —
From the same source I have not taken
My sorrow — I could not awaken
My heart to joy at the same tone —
And all I lov'd — *I* lov'd alone —
Then — in my childhood — in the dawn
Of a most stormy life — was drawn
From ev'ry depth of good and ill
The mystery which binds me still —
From the torrent, or the fountain —
From the red cliff of the mountain —
From the sun that 'round me roll'd
In its autumn tint of gold —
From the lightning in the sky
As it pass'd me flying by —
From the thunder, and the storm —
And the cloud that took the form
(When the rest of Heaven was blue)
Of a demon in my view —

[1829]

INTRODUCTION

Romance, who loves to nod and sing,
With drowsy head and folded wing,
Among the green leaves as they shake
Far down within some shadowy lake,
To me a painted paroquet
Hath been — a most familiar bird —
Taught me my alphabet to say —
To lisp my very earliest word
While in the wild-wood I did lie
A child — with a most knowing eye.

Succeeding years, too wild for song,
Then roll'd like tropic storms along,
Where, tho' the garish lights that fly
Dying along the troubled sky,
Lay bare, thro' vistas thunder-riven,
The blackness of the general Heaven,
That very blackness yet doth fling
Light on the lightning's silver wing.

For, being an idle boy lang syne,
Who read Anacreon, and drank wine,
I early found Anacreon rhymes
Were almost passionate sometimes —
And by strange alchemy of brain
His pleasures always turn'd to pain —
His naivete to wild desire —
His wit to love — his wine to fire —

And so, being young and dipt in folly
I fell in love with melancholy,
And used to throw my earthly rest
And quiet all away in jest —
I could not love except where Death
Was mingling his with Beauty's breath —
Or Hymen, Time, and Destiny
Were stalking between her and me.

O, then the eternal Condor years
So shook the very Heavens on high,
With tumult as they thunder'd by;
I had no time for idle cares,
Thro' gazing on the unquiet sky!
Or if an hour with calmer wing
Its down did on my spirit fling,
That little hour with lyre and rhyme
To while away — forbidden thing!
My heart half fear'd to be a crime
Unless it trembled with the string.

But *now* my soul hath too much room —
Gone are the glory and the gloom —
The black hath mellow'd into grey,
And all the fires are fading away.

My draught of passion hath been deep —
I revell'd, and I now would sleep —
And after-drunkenness of soul
Succeeds the glories of the bowl —

An idle longing night and day
To dream my very life away.

But dreams — of those who dream as I,
Aspiringly, are damned, and die:
Yet should I swear I mean alone,
By notes so very shrilly blown,
To break upon Time's monotone,
While yet my vapid joy and grief
Are tintless of the yellow leaf —
Why not an imp the greybeard hath,
Will shake his shadow in my path —
And even the greybeard will o'erlook
Connivingly my dreaming-book.

[1829–1831]

TO HELEN

Helen, thy beauty is to me
  Like those Nicéan barks of yore,
That gently, o'er a perfumed sea,
  The weary, way-worn wanderer bore
  To his own native shore.

On desperate seas long wont to roam,
  Thy hyacinth hair, thy classic face,
Thy Naiad airs have brought me home
  To the glory that was Greece,
And the grandeur that was Rome.

Lo! in yon brilliant window-niche
  How statue-like I see thee stand,
  The agate lamp within thy hand!
Ah, Psyche, from the regions which
  Are Holy-Land!

[1831–1843]

ISRAFEL

And the angel Israfel, whose heart-strings are a lute, and who has the sweetest voice of all God's creatures.
—KORAN.

In Heaven a spirit doth dwell
  "Whose heart-strings are a lute;"
None sing so wildly well
As the angel Israfel,
And the giddy stars (so legends tell)
Ceasing their hymns, attend the spell
  Of his voice, all mute.

Tottering above
  In her highest noon,
  The enamoured moon
Blushes with love,
  While, to listen, the red levin
  (With the rapid Pleiads, even,
  Which were seven,)
  Pauses in Heaven.

And they say (the starry choir
  And the other listening things)
That Israfeli's fire
Is owing to that lyre
  By which he sits and sings —
The trembling living wire
Of those unusual strings.

But the skies that angel trod,
  Where deep thoughts are a duty —
Where Love's a grown-up God —
  Where the Houri glances are
Imbued with all the beauty
  Which we worship in a star.

Therefore, thou art not wrong,
  Israfeli, who despisest
An unimpassioned song;
To thee the laurels belong,
  Best bard, because the wisest!
Merrily live, and long!

The ecstasies above
  With thy burning measures suit —
Thy grief, thy joy, thy hate, thy love,
  With the fervour of thy lute —
  Well may the stars be mute!

Yes, Heaven is thine; but this
  Is a world of sweets and sours;
  Our flowers are merely — flowers,
And the shadow of thy perfect bliss
  Is the sunshine of ours.

If I could dwell
Where Israfel
  Hath dwelt, and he where I,
He might not sing so wildly well

A mortal melody,
While a bolder note than this might swell
From my lyre within the sky.

[1831–1845]

THE VALLEY OF UNREST

Once it smiled a silent dell
Where the people did not dwell;
They had gone unto the wars,
Trusting to the mild-eyed stars,
Nightly, from their azure towers,
To keep watch above the flowers,
In the midst of which all day
The red sun-light lazily lay.
Now each visiter shall confess
The sad valley's restlessness.
Nothing there is motionless.
Nothing save the airs that brood
Over the magic solitude.
Ah, by no wind are stirred those trees
That palpitate like the chill seas
Around the misty Hebrides!
Ah, by no wind those clouds are driven
That rustle through the unquiet Heaven
Uneasily, from morn till even,
Over the violets there that lie
In myriad types of the human eye —
Over the lilies there that wave
And weep above a nameless grave!
They wave: — from out their fragrant tops
Eternal dews come down in drops.
They weep: — from off their delicate stems
Perennial tears descend in gems.

[1831–1845]

THE CITY IN THE SEA

Lo! Death has reared himself a throne
In a strange city lying alone
Far down within the dim West,
Where the good and the bad and the worst and
  the best
Have gone to their eternal rest.
There shrines and palaces and towers
(Time-eaten towers that tremble not!)
Resemble nothing that is ours.
Around, by lifting winds forgot,
Resignedly beneath the sky
The melancholy waters lie.

No rays from the holy heaven come down
On the long night-time of that town;
But light from out the lurid sea
Streams up the turrets silently —
Gleams up the pinnacles far and free
Up domes — up spires — up kingly halls —
Up fanes — up Babylon-like walls —
Up shadowy long-forgotten bowers
Of sculptured ivy and stone flowers —
Up many and many a marvellous shrine
Whose wreathéd friezes intertwine
The viol, the violet, and the vine.

Resignedly beneath the sky
The melancholy waters lie.
So blend the turrets and shadows there

That all seem pendulous in air,
While from a proud tower in the town
Death looks gigantically down.

There open fanes and gaping graves
Yawn level with the luminous waves·
But not the riches there that lie
In each idol's diamond eye —
Not the gaily-jewelled dead
Tempt the waters from their bed;
For no ripples curl, alas!
Along that wilderness of glass —
No swellings tell that winds may be
Upon some far-off happier sea —
No heavings hint that winds have been
On seas less hideously serene.

But lo, a stir is in the air!
The wave — there is a movement there!
As if the towers had thrust aside,
In slightly sinking, the dull tide —
As if their tops had feebly given
A void within the filmy Heaven.
The waves have now a redder glow —
The hours are breathing faint and low —
And when, amid no earthly moans,
Down, down that town shall settle hence,
Hell, rising from a thousand thrones,
Shall do it reverence.

[1831–1845]

TO ONE IN PARADISE

Thou wast that all to me, love,
  For which my soul did pine —
A green isle in the sea, love,
  A fountain and a shrine,
All wreathed with fairy fruits and flowers,
  And all the flowers were mine.

Ah, dream too bright to last!
  Ah, starry Hope! that didst arise
But to be overcast!
  A voice from out the Future cries,
"On! on!" — but o'er the Past
  (Dim gulf!) my spirit hovering lies
Mute, motionless, aghast!

For, alas! alas! with me
  The light of Life is o'er!
  No more — no more — no more —
(Such language holds the solemn sea
  To the sands upon the shore)
Shall bloom the thunder-blasted tree,
  Or the stricken eagle soar!

And all my days are trances,
  And all my nightly dreams
Are where thy grey eye glances,
  And where thy footstep gleams —
In what ethereal dances,
By what eternal streams.

[1833–1849]

THE COLISEUM

Type of the antique Rome! Rich reliquary
Of lofty contemplation left to Time
By buried centuries of pomp and power!
At length — at length — after so many days
Of weary pilgrimage and burning thirst,
(Thirst for the springs of lore that in thee lie,)
I kneel, an altered and an humble man,
Amid thy shadows, and so drink within
My very soul thy grandeur, gloom and glory!

Vastness! and Age! and Memories of Eld!
Silence! and Desolation! and dim Night!
I feel ye now — I feel ye in your strength —
O spells more sure than e'er Judæan king
Taught in the gardens of Gethsemane!
O charms more potent than the rapt Chaldee
Ever drew down from out the quiet stars!

Here, where a hero fell, a column falls!
Here, where the mimic eagle glared in gold,
A midnight vigil holds the swarthy bat!
Here, where the dames of Rome their gilded hair
Waved to the wind, now wave the reed and thistle!
Here, where on golden throne the monarch lolled,
Glides, spectre-like, unto his marble home,
Lit by the wan light of the horned moon,

The swift and silent lizard of the stones!

But stay! these walls — these ivy-clad
  arcades —
These mouldering plinths — these sad and
  blackened shafts —
These vague entablatures — this crumbling
  frieze —
These shattered cornices — this wreck — this
  ruin —
These stones — alas! these gray stones — are
  they all —
All of the famed, and the colossal left
By the corrosive Hours to Fate and me?

"Not all" — the Echoes answer me — "not all!
"Prophetic sounds and loud, arise forever
"From us, and from all Ruin, unto the wise,
"As melody from Memnon to the Sun.
"We rule the hearts of mightiest men — we rule
"With a despotic sway all giant minds.
"We are not impotent — we pallid stones.
"Not all our power is gone — not all our fame —
"Not all the magic of our high renown —
"Not all the wonder that encircles us —
"Not all the mysteries that in us lie —
"Not all the memories that hang upon
"And cling around about us as a garment,
"Clothing us in a robe of more than glory."

[1833–1843]

THE HAUNTED PALACE

In the greenest of our valleys
  By good angels tenanted,
Once a fair and stately palace —
  Radiant palace — reared its head.
In the monarch Thought's dominion —
  It stood there!
Never seraph spread a pinion
  Over fabric half so fair!

Banners yellow, glorious, golden,
  On its roof did float and flow —
(This — all this — was in the olden
  Time long ago)
And every gentle air that dallied,
  In that sweet day,
Along the ramparts plumed and pallid,
  A wingéd odor went away.

Wanderers in that happy valley,
  Through two luminous windows, saw
Spirits moving musically,
  To a lute's well-tunéd law,
Round about a throne where, sitting,
  Porphyrogene,
In state his glory well befitting
  The ruler of the realm was seen.

And all with pearl and ruby glowing
  Was the fair palace door,

Through which came flowing, flowing, flowing,
  And sparkling evermore,
A troop of Echoes whose sweet duty
  Was but to sing,
In voices of surpassing beauty,
  The wit and wisdom of their king.

But evil things, in robes of sorrow,
  Assailed the monarch's high estate.
(Ah, let us mourn! — for never morrow
  Shall dawn upon him, desolate!)
And round about his home the glory
  That blushed and bloomed,
Is but a dim-remembered story
  Of the old-time entombed.

And travelers, now, within that valley,
  Through the encrimsoned windows see
Vast forms that move fantastically
  To a discordant melody,
While, like a ghastly rapid river,
  Through the pale door
A hideous throng rush out forever
  And laugh — but smile no more.

[1838–1848]

THE CONQUEROR WORM

Lo! 'tis a gala night
  Within the lonesome latter years!
An angel throng, bewinged, bedight
  In veils, and drowned in tears,
Sit in a theatre, to see
  A play of hopes and fears,
While the orchestra breathes fitfully
  The music of the spheres.

Mimes, in the form of God on high,
  Mutter and mumble low,
And hither and thither fly —
  Mere puppets they, who come and go
At bidding of vast formless things
  That shift the scenery to and fro,
Flapping from out their Condor wings
  Invisible Wo!

That motley drama — oh, be sure
  It shall not be forgot!
With its Phantom chased for evermore,
  By a crowd that seize it not,
Through a circle that ever returneth in
  To the self-same spot,
And much of Madness, and more of Sin
  And Horror the soul of the plot.

But see, amid the mimic rout
  A crawling shape intrude!

A blood-red thing that writhes from out
  The scenic solitude!
It writhes! — it writhes! — with mortal pangs
  The mimes become its food,
And seraphs sob at vermin fangs
  In human gore imbued.

Out — out are the lights — out all!
  And, over each quivering form,
The curtain, a funeral pall,
  Comes down with the rush of a storm,
While the angels, all pallid and wan,
  Uprising, unveiling, affirm
That the play is the tragedy, "Man,"
  And its hero the Conqueror Worm.

[1842–1849]

DREAM-LAND

By a route obscure and lonely,
Haunted by ill angels only,
Where an Eidolon, named Night,
On a black throne reigns upright,
I have reached these lands but newly
From an ultimate dim Thule —
From a wild weird clime that lieth, sublime,
Out of Space — out of Time.

Bottomless vales and boundless floods,
And chasms, and caves, and Titan woods,
With forms that no man can discover
For the dews that drip all over;
Mountains toppling evermore
Into seas without a shore;
Seas that restlessly aspire,
Surging, unto skies of fire;
Lakes that endlessly outspread
Their lone waters — lone and dead, —
Their still waters — still and chilly
With the snows of the lolling lily.

By the lakes that thus outspread
Their lone waters, lone and dead, —
Their sad waters, sad and chilly
With the snows of the lolling lily, —
By the mountains — near the river
Murmuring lowly, murmuring ever, —
By the grey woods, — by the swamp
Where the toad and the newt encamp, —

By the dismal tarns and pools
Where dwell the Ghouls, —
By each spot the most unholy —
In each nook most melancholy, —
There the traveller meets aghast
Sheeted Memories of the Past —
Shrouded forms that start and sigh
As they pass the wanderer by —
White-robed forms of friends long given,
In agony, to the Earth — and Heaven.

For the heart whose woes are legion
'Tis a peaceful, soothing region —
For the spirit that walks in shadow
O! it is an Eldorado!
But the traveller, travelling through it,
May not — dare not openly view it;
Never its mysteries are exposed
To the weak human eye unclosed;
So wills its King, who hath forbid
The uplifting of the fringed lid;
And thus the sad Soul that here passes
Beholds it but through darkened glasses.

By a route obscure and lonely,
Haunted by ill angels only,
Where an Eidolon, named NIGHT,
On a black throne reigns upright,
I have wandered home but newly
From this ultimate dim Thule.

[1844–1849]

EULALIE

I dwelt alone
In a world of moan,
And my soul was a stagnant tide
Till the fair and gentle Eulalie became my
blushing bride —
Till the yellow-haired young Eulalie became my
smiling bride.

Ah, less, less bright
The stars of the night
Than the eyes of the radiant girl,
And never a flake
That the vapor can make
With the moon-tints of purple and pearl
Can vie with the modest Eulalie's most
unregarded curl —
Can compare with the bright-eyed Eulalie's
most humble and careless curl.

Now Doubt — now Pain
Come never again,
For her soul gives me sigh for sigh
And all day long
Shines bright and strong
Astarté within the sky,
While ever to her dear Eulalie upturns her
matron eye —
While ever to her young Eulalie upturns her
violet eye.

[1844–1845]

THE RAVEN

Once upon a midnight dreary, while I pondered,
weak and weary,
Over many a quaint and curious volume of
forgotten lore —
While I nodded, nearly napping, suddenly there
came a tapping,
As of some one gently rapping, rapping at my
chamber door —
" 'Tis some visiter," I muttered, "tapping at my
chamber door —
Only this and nothing more."

Ah, distinctly I remember it was in the bleak
December;
And each separate dying ember wrought its
ghost upon the floor.
Eagerly I wished the morrow; — vainly I had
sought to borrow
From my books surcease of sorrow — sorrow for
the lost Lenore —
For the rare and radiant maiden whom the
angels name Lenore —
Nameless *here* for evermore.

And the silken, sad, uncertain rustling of each
purple curtain
Thrilled me — filled me with fantastic terrors
never felt before;

So that now, to still the beating of my heart, I stood repeating
" 'Tis some visiter entreating entrance at my chamber door —
Some late visiter entreating entrance at my chamber door; —
This it is and nothing more."

Presently my soul grew stronger; hesitating then no longer,
"Sir," said I, "or Madam, truly your forgiveness I implore;
But the fact is I was napping, and so gently you came rapping,
And so faintly you came tapping, tapping at my chamber door,
That I scarce was sure I heard you" — here I opened wide the door; ———
Darkness there and nothing more.

Deep into that darkness peering, long I stood there wondering, fearing,
Doubting, dreaming dreams no mortal ever dared to dream before;
But the silence was unbroken, and the stillness gave no token,
And the only word there spoken was the whispered word, "Lenore?"
This I whispered, and an echo murmured back the word, "Lenore!"
Merely this and nothing more.

Back into the chamber turning, all my soul
within me burning,
Soon again I heard a tapping somewhat louder
than before.
"Surely," said I, "surely that is something at my
window lattice;
Let me see, then, what thereat is, and this
mystery explore —
Let my heart be still a moment and this
mystery explore; —
'Tis the wind and nothing more!"

Open here I flung the shutter, when, with many
a flirt and flutter,
In there stepped a stately Raven of the saintly
days of yore;
Not the least obeisance made he; not a minute
stopped or stayed he;
But, with mien of lord or lady, perched above
my chamber door —
Perched upon a bust of Pallas just above my
chamber door —
Perched, and sat, and nothing more.

Then this ebony bird beguiling my sad fancy
into smiling,
By the grave and stern decorum of the
countenance it wore,
"Though thy crest be shorn and shaven, thou," I
said, "art sure no craven,
Ghastly grim and ancient Raven wandering

from the Nightly shore —
Tell me what thy lordly name is on the Night's Plutonian shore!"
Quoth the Raven "Nevermore."

Much I marvelled this ungainly fowl to hear discourse so plainly.
Though its answer little meaning — little relevancy bore;
For we cannot help agreeing that no living human being
Ever yet was blessed with seeing bird above his chamber door —
Bird or beast upon the sculptured bust above his chamber door,
With such name as "Nevermore."

But the Raven, sitting lonely on the placid bust, spoke only
That one word, as if his soul in that one word he did outpour.
Nothing farther then he uttered — not a feather then he fluttered —
Till I scarcely more than muttered "Other friends have flown before —
On the morrow *he* will leave me, as my Hopes have flown before."
Then the bird said "Nevermore."

Startled at the stillness broken by reply so aptly spoken,

"Doubtless," said I, "what it utters is its only
stock and store
Caught from some unhappy master whom
unmerciful Disaster
Followed fast and followed faster till his songs
one burden bore —
Till the dirges of his Hope that melancholy
burden bore
Of 'Never — nevermore.' "

But the Raven still beguiling my sad fancy into
smiling,
Straight I wheeled a cushioned seat in front of
bird, and bust and door;
Then, upon the velvet sinking, I betook myself
to linking
Fancy unto fancy, thinking what this ominous
bird of yore —
What this grim, ungainly, ghastly, gaunt, and
ominous bird of yore
Meant in croaking "Nevermore."

This I sat engaged in guessing, but no syllable
expressing
To the fowl whose fiery eyes now burned into
my bosom's core;
This and more I sat divining, with my head at
ease reclining
On the cushion's velvet lining that the lamp-
light gloated o'er,

But whose velvet-violet lining with the lamp-
light gloating o'er,
She shall press, ah, nevermore!

Then, methought, the air grew denser,
perfumed from an unseen censer
Swung by seraphim whose foot-falls tinkled on
the tufted floor.
"Wretch," I cried, "thy God hath lent thee — by
these angels he hath sent thee
Respite — respite and nepenthe from thy
memories of Lenore;
Quaff, oh quaff this kind nepenthe and forget
this lost Lenore!"
Quoth the Raven "Nevermore."

"Prophet!" said I, "thing of evil! — prophet still,
if bird or devil! —
Whether Tempter sent, or whether tempest
tossed thee here ashore,
Desolate yet all undaunted, on this desert land
enchanted —
On this home by Horror haunted — tell me
truly, I implore —
Is there — *is* there balm in Gilead? — tell me —
tell me, I implore!"
Quoth the Raven "Nevermore."

"Prophet!" said I, "thing of evil! — prophet still,
if bird or devil!

By that Heaven that bends above us — by that
God we both adore —
Tell this soul with sorrow laden if, within the
distant Aidenn,
It shall clasp a sainted maiden whom the angels
name Lenore —
Clasp a rare and radiant maiden whom the
angels name Lenore."
Quoth the Raven "Nevermore."

"Be that word our sign of parting, bird or fiend!"
I shrieked, upstarting —
"Get thee back into the tempest and the Night's
Plutonian shore!
Leave no black plume as a token of that lie thy
soul hath spoken!
Leave my loneliness unbroken! — quit the bust
above my door!
Take thy beak from out my heart, and take thy
form from off my door!"
Quoth the Raven "Nevermore."

And the Raven, never flitting, still is sitting,
still is sitting
On the pallid bust of Pallas just above my
chamber door;
And his eyes have all the seeming of a demon's
that is dreaming,
And the lamp-light o'er him streaming throws
his shadow on the floor;

And my soul from out that shadow that lies
floating on the floor
Shall be lifted — nevermore!

[1844–1849]

[“DEEP IN EARTH”]

Deep in earth my love is lying
And I must weep alone.

[1847]

TO M. L. S——

Of all who hail thy presence as the morning —
Of all to whom thine absence is the night —
The blotting utterly from out high heaven
The sacred sun — of all who, weeping, bless thee
Hourly for hope — for life — ah! above all,
For the resurrection of deep-buried faith
In Truth — in Virtue — in Humanity —
Of all who, on Despair's unhallowed bed
Lying down to die, have suddenly arisen
At thy soft-murmured words, "Let there be light!"
At the soft-murmured words that were fulfilled
In the seraphic glancing of thine eyes —
Of all who owe thee most — whose gratitude
Nearest resembles worship — oh, remember
The truest — the most fervently devoted,
And think that these weak lines are written by him —
By him who, as he pens them, thrills to think
His spirit is communing with an angel's.

[1847]

ULALUME — A BALLAD

The skies they were ashen and sober;
  The leaves they were crispéd and sere —
  The leaves they were withering and sere:
It was night, in the lonesome October
  Of my most immemorial year:
It was hard by the dim lake of Auber,
  In the misty mid region of Weir: —
It was down by the dank tarn of Auber,
  In the ghoul-haunted woodland of Weir.

Here once, through an alley Titanic,
  Of cypress, I roamed with my Soul —
  Of cypress, with Psyche, my Soul.
These were days when my heart was volcanic
  As the scoriac rivers that roll —
  As the lavas that restlessly roll
Their sulphurous currents down Yaanek,
  In the ultimate climes of the Pole —
That groan as they roll down Mount Yaanek,
  In the realms of the Boreal Pole.

Our talk had been serious and sober,
  But our thoughts they were palsied and sere —
  Our memories were treacherous and sere;
For we knew not the month was October,
  And we marked not the night of the year —
  (Ah, night of all nights in the year!)
We noted not the dim lake of Auber,
  (Though once we had journeyed down here)

We remembered not the dank tarn of Auber,
  Nor the ghoul-haunted woodland of Weir.

And now, as the night was senescent,
  And star-dials pointed to morn —
  As the star-dials hinted of morn —
At the end of our path a liquescent
  And nebulous lustre was born,
Out of which a miraculous crescent
  Arose with a duplicate horn —
Astarte's bediamonded crescent,
  Distinct with its duplicate horn.

And I said — "She is warmer than Dian;
  She rolls through an ether of sighs —
  She revels in a region of sighs.
She has seen that the tears are not dry on
  These cheeks where the worm never dies,
And has come past the stars of the Lion,
  To point us the path to the skies —
  To the Lethean peace of the skies —
Come up, in despite of the Lion,
  To shine on us with her bright eyes —
Come up, through the lair of the Lion,
  With love in her luminous eyes."

But Psyche, uplifting her finger,
  Said — "Sadly this star I mistrust —
  Her pallor I strangely mistrust —
Ah, hasten! — ah, let us not linger!
  Ah, fly! — let us fly! — for we must."

In terror she spoke; letting sink her
  Wings till they trailed in the dust —
In agony sobbed; letting sink her
  Plumes till they trailed in the dust —
  Till they sorrowfully trailed in the dust.

I replied — "This is nothing but dreaming.
  Let us on, by this tremulous light!
  Let us bathe in this crystalline light!
Its Sibyllic splendor is beaming
  With Hope and in Beauty to-night —
  See! — it flickers up the sky through the night!
Ah, we safely may trust to its gleaming
  And be sure it will lead us aright —
We surely may trust to a gleaming
    That cannot but guide us aright
Since it flickers up to Heaven through the
  night."

Thus I pacified Psyche and kissed her,
  And tempted her out of her gloom —
  And conquered her scruples and gloom;
And we passed to the end of the vista —
  But were stopped by the door of a tomb —
  By the door of a legended tomb: —
And I said — "What is written, sweet sister,
  On the door of this legended tomb?"
  She replied — "Ulalume — Ulalume! —
  'T is the vault of thy lost Ulalume!"

Then my heart it grew ashen and sober

As the leaves that were crispéd and sere —
As the leaves that were withering and sere —
And I cried — "It was surely October,
On *this* very night of last year,
That I journeyed — I journeyed down here! —
That I brought a dread burden down here —
On this night, of all nights in the year,
Ah, what demon hath tempted me here?
Well I know, now, this dim lake of Auber —
This misty mid region of Weir: —
Well I know, now, this dank tarn of Auber —
This ghoul-haunted woodland of Weir."

Said we, then — the two, then — "Ah, can it
Have been that the woodlandish ghouls —
The pitiful, the merciful ghouls,
To bar up our way and to ban it
From the secret that lies in these wolds —
From the thing that lies hidden in these
wolds —
Have drawn up the spectre of a planet
From the limbo of lunary souls —
This sinfully scintillant planet
From the Hell of the planetary souls?"

[1847–1849]

THE BELLS

1.

Hear the sledges with the bells —
Silver bells!
What a world of merriment their melody foretells!
How they tinkle, tinkle, tinkle,
In the icy air of night!
While the stars that oversprinkle
All the Heavens, seem to twinkle
With a crystalline delight;
Keeping time, time, time,
In a sort of Runic rhyme,
To the tintinabulation that so musically wells
From the bells, bells, bells, bells,
Bells, bells, bells —
From the jingling and the tinkling of the bells.

2.

Hear the mellow wedding bells —
Golden bells!
What a world of happiness their harmony foretells!
Through the balmy air of night
How they ring out their delight! —
From the molten-golden notes
And all in tune,
What a liquid ditty floats
To the turtle-dove that listens while she gloats
On the moon!
Oh, from out the sounding cells
What a gush of euphony voluminously wells!

How it swells!
How it dwells
On the Future! — how it tells
Of the rapture that impels
To the swinging and the ringing
Of the bells, bells, bells! —
Of the bells, bells, bells, bells,
Bells, bells, bells —
To the rhyming and the chiming of the bells!

3.

Hear the loud alarum bells —
Brazen bells!
What tale of terror, now, their turbulency tells!
In the startled ear of Night
How they scream out their affright!
Too much horrified to speak,
They can only shriek, shriek,
Out of tune,
In a clamorous appealing to the mercy of the fire —
In a mad expostulation with the deaf and frantic fire,
Leaping higher, higher, higher,
With a desperate desire
And a resolute endeavor
Now — now to sit, or never,
By the side of the pale-faced moon.
Oh, the bells, bells, bells!
What a tale their terror tells
Of despair!
How they clang and clash and roar!
What a horror they outpour

In the bosom of the palpitating air!
Yet the ear, it fully knows,
By the twanging
And the clanging,
How the danger ebbs and flows: —
Yes, the ear distinctly tells,
In the jangling
And the wrangling,
How the danger sinks and swells,
By the sinking or the swelling in the anger of the bells -
Of the bells —
Of the bells, bells, bells, bells,
Bells, bells, bells —
In the clamor and the clangor of the bells.

4.

Hear the tolling of the bells —
Iron bells!
What a world of solemn thought their monody compels!
In the silence of the night
How we shiver with affright
At the melancholy meaning of the tone!
For every sound that floats
From the rust within their throats
Is a groan.
And the people — ah, the people
They that dwell up in the steeple
All alone,
And who, tolling, tolling, tolling,
In that muffled monotone,
Feel a glory in so rolling

On the human heart a stone —
They are neither man nor woman —
They are neither brute nor human,
They are Ghouls: —
And their king it is who tolls: —
And he rolls, rolls, rolls, rolls
A Pæan from the bells!
And his merry bosom swells
With the Pæan of the bells!
And he dances and he yells;
Keeping time, time, time,
In a sort of Runic rhyme,
To the Pæan of the bells —
Of the bells: —
Keeping time, time, time,
In a sort of Runic rhyme,
To the throbbing of the bells —
Of the bells, bells, bells —
To the sobbing of the bells: —
Keeping time, time, time,
As he knells, knells, knells,
In a happy Runic rhyme,
To the rolling of the bells —
Of the bells, bells, bells: —
To the tolling of the bells —
Of the bells, bells, bells, bells,
Bells, bells, bells —
To the moaning and the groaning of the bells.

[July 1849]

TO HELEN [WHITMAN]

I saw thee once — once only — years ago:
I must not say *how* many — but *not* many.
It was a July midnight; and from out
A full-orbed moon, that, like thine own soul,
soaring,
Sought a precipitate pathway up through
heaven,
There fell a silvery-silken veil of light,
With quietude, and sultriness, and slumber,
Upon the upturn'd faces of a thousand
Roses that grew in an enchanted garden,
Where no wind dared to stir, unless on tiptoe —
Fell on the upturn'd faces of these roses
That gave out, in return for the love-light,
Their odorous souls in an ecstatic death —
Fell on the upturn'd faces of these roses
That smiled and died in this parterre,
enchanted
By thee, and by the poetry of thy presence.

Clad all in white, upon a violet bank
I saw thee half reclining; while the moon
Fell on the upturn'd faces of the roses,
And on thine own, upturn'd — alas, in sorrow!

Was it not Fate, that, on this July midnight —
Was it not Fate, (whose name is also Sorrow,)
That bade me pause before that garden-gate,

To breathe the incense of those slumbering
roses?
No footstep stirred: the hated world all slept,
Save only thee and me. (Oh, Heaven! — oh,
God!
How my heart beats in coupling those two
words!)
Save only thee and me. I paused — I looked —
And in an instant all things disappeared.
(Ah, bear in mind this garden was enchanted!)
The pearly lustre of the moon went out:
The mossy banks and the meandering paths,
The happy flowers and the repining trees,
Were seen no more: the very roses' odors
Died in the arms of the adoring airs.
All — all expired save thee — save less than
thou:
Save only the divine light in thine eyes —
Save but the soul in thine uplifted eyes.
I saw but them — they were the world to me.
I saw but them — saw only them for hours —
Saw only them until the moon went down.
What wild heart-histories seemed to lie
enwritten
Upon those crystalline, celestial spheres!
How dark a wo! yet how sublime a hope!
How silently serene a sea of pride!
How daring an ambition! yet how deep —
How fathomless a capacity for love!
But now, at length, dear Dian sank from sight,

Into a western couch of thunder-cloud;
And thou, a ghost, amid the entombing trees
Didst glide away. *Only thine eyes remained.*
They *would not* go — they never yet have gone.
Lighting my lonely pathway home that night,
They have not left me (as my hopes have) since.
They follow me — they lead me through the
years.
They are my ministers — yet I their slave.
Their office is to illumine and enkindle —
My duty, *to be saved* by their bright light,
And purified in their electric fire,
And sanctified in their elysian fire.
They fill my soul with Beauty (which is Hope,)
And are far up in Heaven — the stars I kneel to
In the sad, silent watches of my night;
While even in the meridian glare of day
I see them still — two sweetly scintillant
Venuses, unextinguished by the sun!

[1848–1849]

A DREAM WITHIN A DREAM

Take this kiss upon the brow!
And, in parting from you now,
Thus much let me avow —
You are not wrong, who deem
That my days have been a dream;
Yet if hope has flown away
In a night, or in a day,
In a vision, or in none,
Is it therefore the less *gone*?
All that we see or seem
Is but a dream within a dream.

I stand amid the roar
Of a surf-tormented shore,
And I hold within my hand
Grains of the golden sand —
How few! yet how they creep
Through my fingers to the deep,
While I weep — while I weep!
O God! can I not grasp
Them with a tighter clasp?
O God! can I not save
One from the pitiless wave?
Is *all* that we see or seem
But a dream within a dream?

[1849]

FOR ANNIE

Thank Heaven! the crisis —
  The danger is past,
And the lingering illness
  Is over at last —
And the fever called "Living"
  Is conquered at last.

Sadly, I know
  I am shorn of my strength,
And no muscle I move
  As I lie at full length —
But no matter! — I feel
  I am better at length.

And I rest so composedly,
  Now, in my bed,
That any beholder
  Might fancy me dead —
Might start at beholding me,
  Thinking me dead.

The moaning and groaning,
  The sighing and sobbing,
Are quieted now,
  With that horrible throbbing
At heart: — ah, that horrible,
  Horrible throbbing!

The sickness — the nausea —

The pitiless pain —
Have ceased, with the fever
That maddened my brain —
With the fever called 'Living'
That burned in my brain.

And oh! of all tortures
That torture the worst
Has abated — the terrible
Torture of thirst
For the napthaline river
Of Passion accurst: —
I have drank of a water
That quenches all thirst —

Of a water that flows,
With a lullaby sound,
From a spring but a very few
Feet under ground —
From a cavern not very far
Down under ground.

And ah! let it never
Be foolishly said
That my room it is gloomy
And narrow my bed;
For man never slept
In a different bed —
And, to *sleep*, you must slumber
In just such a bed.

My tantalized spirit
  Here blandly reposes,
Forgetting, or never
  Regretting its roses —
Its old agitations
  Of myrtles and roses:

For now, while so quietly
  Lying, it fancies
A holier odor
  About it, of pansies —
A rosemary odor,
  Commingled with pansies —
With rue and the beautiful
  Puritan pansies.

And so it lies happily,
  Bathing in many
A dream of the truth
  And the beauty of Annie —
Drowned in a bath
  Of the tresses of Annie.

She tenderly kissed me,
  She fondly caressed,
And then I fell gently
  To sleep on her breast —
Deeply to sleep
  From the heaven of her breast.

When the light was extinguished,
  She covered me warm,
And she prayed to the angels
  To keep me from harm —
To the queen of the angels
  To shield me from harm.

And I lie so composedly,
  Now, in my bed,
(Knowing her love)
  That you fancy me dead —
And I rest so contentedly,
  Now in my bed,
(With her love at my breast)
  That you fancy me dead —
That you shudder to look at me,
  Thinking me dead: —

But my heart it is brighter
  Than all of the many
Stars in the sky,
  For it sparkles with Annie —
It glows with the light
  Of the love of my Annie —
With the thought of the light
  Of the eyes of my Annie.

[1849]

ELDORADO

Gaily bedight,
A gallant knight,
In sunshine and in shadow,
Had journeyed long,
Singing a song,
In search of Eldorado.

But he grew old —
This knight so bold —
And o'er his heart a shadow
Fell, as he found
No spot of ground
That looked like Eldorado.

And, as his strength
Failed him at length
He met a pilgrim shadow —
"Shadow," said he,
"Where can it be —
This land of Eldorado?"

"Over the Mountains
Of the Moon,
Down the Valley of the Shadow,
Ride, boldly ride,"
The shade replied, —
"If you seek for Eldorado!"

[1849]

TO MY MOTHER

Because I feel that, in the Heavens above,
  The angels, whispering to one another,
Can find, among their burning terms of love,
  None so devotional as that of "Mother,"
Therefore by that dear name I long have called
    you —
  You who are more than mother unto me,
And fill my heart of hearts, where Death
    installed you
  In setting my Virginia's spirit free.
My mother — my own mother, who died early,
  Was but the mother of myself; but you
Are mother to the one I loved so dearly,
  And thus are dearer than the mother I knew
By that infinity with which my wife
  Was dearer to my soul than its soul-life.

[1849]

ANNABEL LEE

It was many and many a year ago,
  In a kingdom by the sea,
That a maiden there lived whom you may know
  By the name of Annabel Lee; —
And this maiden she lived with no other
  thought
  Than to love and be loved by me.

I was a child and *she* was a child,
  In this kingdom by the sea;
But we loved with a love that was more than
  love —
  I and my Annabel Lee —
With a love that the wingéd seraphs in Heaven
  Coveted her and me.

And this was the reason that, long ago,
  In this kingdom by the sea,
A wind blew out of a cloud, chilling
  My beautiful Annabel Lee;
So that her high-born kinsmen came
  And bore her away from me,
To shut her up in a sepulchre,
  In this kingdom by the sea.

The angels, not half so happy in Heaven,
  Went envying her and me —
Yes! — that was the reason (as all men know,
  In this kingdom by the sea)

That the wind came out of the cloud by night,
  Chilling and killing my Annabel Lee.

But our love it was stronger by far than the love
  Of those who were older than we —
  Of many far wiser than we —
And neither the angels in Heaven above,
  Nor the demons down under the sea,
Can ever dissever my soul from the soul
  Of the beautiful Annabel Lee: —

For the moon never beams, without bringing me dreams
  Of the beautiful Annabel Lee;
And the stars never rise, but I feel the bright eyes
  Of the beautiful Annabel Lee: —
And so, all the night-tide, I lie down by the side
Of my darling — my darling — my life and my bride,
  In her sepulchre there by the sea —
  In her tomb by the sounding sea.

[May 1849]

INDEX OF FIRST LINES

Because I feel that, in the Heavens above, 63

By a route obscure and lonely, 33

Deep in earth my love is lying 44

From childhood's hour I have not been 15

Gaily bedight, 62

Hear the sledges with the bells — 50

Helen, thy beauty is to me 19

I dwelt alone 35

I saw thee once — once only — years ago: 54

In Heaven a spirit doth dwell 20

In the greenest of our valleys 29

In youth's spring, it was my lot 13

It was many and many a year ago, 64

Lo! Death has reared himself a throne 24

Lo! 'tis a gala night 31

Of all who hail thy presence as the morning — 45

Oh! that my young life were a lasting dream! 11

Once it smiled a silent dell 23

Once upon a midnight dreary, while I pondered, weak and weary, 36

Romance, who loves to nod and sing, 16

Science! true daughter of Old Time thou art! 14

Take this kiss upon the brow! 57

Thank Heaven! the crisis — 58

The skies they were ashen and sober; 46

Thou wast that all to me, love, 26

Type of the antique Rome! Rich reliquary 27

INDEX OF POEMS

[Alone] 15

Annabel Lee 64

The Bells 50

The City in the Sea 24

The Coliseum 27

The Conqueror Worm 31

["Deep in Earth"] 44

Dream-Land 33

Dreams 11

A Dream Within a Dream 57

Eldorado 62

Eulalie 35

For Annie 58

The Haunted Palace 29

Introduction 16

Israfel 20

The Lake 13

The Raven 36

Sonnet—To Science 14

To Helen 19

To Helen [Whitman] 54

To M. L. S—— 45

To My Mother 63

To One in Pardise 26

Ulalume—A Ballad 46

The Valley of Unrest 23

FOR FURTHER INFORMATION

Readers wishing to explore further the writings of Edgar Allan Poe may wish to consult the following editions:

Mabbot, Thomas Ollive, ed. *Collected Works of Edgar Allan Poe*. 3 vols. Cambridge: Harvard University Press, 1969–78.

Pollin, Burton R., ed. *Collected Writings of Edgar Allan Poe*. 4 vols. to date. Boston: Twayne, 1981; New York: Gordian Press, 1985–.

Ostrom, John Ward, ed. *The Letters of Edgar Allan Poe*. rev. ed. 2 vols. New York: Gordian Press, 1966.

Those wishing to learn more about Poe's life may wish to examine the following biographical works:

Allen, Hervey. *Israfel—The Life and Times of Edgar Allan Poe*. New York: Farrar & Rinehart, 1934.

Quinn, Arthur Hobson. *Edgar Allan Poe—A Critical Biography*. New York: D. Appleton-Century, 1941.

Silverman, Kenneth. *Edgar A. Poe—Mournful and Never-ending Remembrance*. New York: HarperCollins, 1991.

Thomas, Dwight, and David K. Jackson. *The Poe Log—A Documentary Life of Edgar Allan Poe 1809–1849*. Boston: G. K. Hall, 1987.

The following periodicals concern Poe's life and writing:

The Poe Messenger (The Poe Museum, 1914–16 East Main Street, Richmond, Virgina 23223).

Poe Studies/Dark Romanticism (Washington State University Press, Pullman, Washington 99164).

Poe Studies Association Newsletter (Poe Studies Association, English Department, Western Oregon State College, Monmouth, Oregon 97361).

The following museums and sites importantly illuminate Poe and his world:

The Poe Museum (1914–16 East Main Street, Richmond, Virginia 23223).

The Poe Cottage (Grand Concourse and Kingsbridge Road, Bronx, New York 10458).

Edgar Allan Poe National Historic Site (532 North 7th Street, Philadelphia, Pennsylvania 19123).

Edgar Allan Poe Room (c/o University Guides Service, The Rotunda, University of Virginia, Charlottesville, Virginia 22903).

Edgar Allan Poe House (203 North Amity Street, Baltimore, Maryland 21223).

Fort Moultrie Visitors Center (1214 Middle Street, Sullivan's Island, South Carolina 29482).

The Casemate Museum (Fort Monroe, Virginia 23651).

The Providence Athenaeum (251 Benefit Street, Providence, Rhode Island 02903).

About the Author

EDGAR ALLAN POE

EDGAR ALLAN POE was born in 1809 in Boston. His parents were itinerant actors, and Poe spent his early life traveling from stage to stage, watching theater from the wings. Poe's father died a year after he was born, his mother shortly thereafter. Three-year-old Edgar was unofficially adopted by a prosperous Virginia couple, John and Frances Allan.

Poe was an intelligent child who succeeded in school, learned several languages, and committed himself to great literature. In 1826, John Allan sent him to the University of Virginia at Charlottesville, where he devoted his life to reading and writing.

After college, Poe wanted to establish himself as a writer but soon realized how costly it was to publish his work. With his adoptive father no longer supporting him, he was forced to join the army to make a living. After leaving the army, Poe became the editor of the *Southern Literary Messenger*, quickly earning a reputation as a respected literary critic.

In January of 1845, Poe published the poem that brought him fame, "The Raven." It was an immediate sensation and made Poe a literary celebrity in his own right.

Some of Poe's other works include *The Narrative of Arthur Gordon Pym, of Nantucket; Tales of the Grotesque and Arabesque*; and many other collections of poetry and short stories.

Edgar Allan Poe will always be remembered for his ability to capture the strange twists of the human mind, and he will endure as one of the greatest literary geniuses of all time.

About the Introduction Author

PHILIP PULLMAN

PHILIP PULLMAN was born in 1946 in Norwich, Norfolk, England. He spent much of his childhood traveling the globe by ship with his family, who lived in Africa and Australia before settling in England. A teacher for many years, Pullman has always been a writer. Pullman's His Dark Materials trilogy — *The Golden Compass, The Subtle Knife,* and *The Amber Spyglass* — is one of the most acclaimed and popular book sequences of all time. His other spellbinding books include *Clockwork, The Ruby in the Smoke,* and *The Firework Maker's Daughter.*